First published in Great Britain 1985 by
Hamish Hamilton Children's Books
Garden House, 57–59 Long Acre, London WC2E 9JZ
Copyright © 1985 by Nigel Snell
All Rights Reserved

British Library Cataloguing in Publication Data

Snell, Nigel
Steve Is Adopted
1. Adoption – Juvenile literature
I. Title
362.7'34   HV875
ISBN 0-241-11511-6

Printed in Great Britain by
Cambus Litho, East Kilbride

Steve Is Adopted

NIGEL SNELL

Hamish Hamilton · London

Steve lived with his mother, his father and his sister Sue.
He was very happy.

When Steve was five years old,
Mummy let him choose a tiny puppy
for his birthday.
Steve decided to call him Rags.

One day, Steve went with Mummy
to the supermarket.
He held tightly on to Rag's lead.

'Oh', said Steve.
'This lady looks like me.'

When they got home, Steve said,
'If you're my mummy,
why aren't you brown?'

Mummy sat on the sofa, and put
her arm around Steve.
'I'll try to explain,' she said.

She told Steve that there were
three ways of joining a family.
You could marry somebody,
you could be born into a family,
or you could be adopted.

Steve had been adopted.
His first Mummy had been brown,
and that was why Steve was brown.

She had loved Steve very much,
but couldn't give him everything
she wanted him to have.
She decided he would be happier
with new parents.

'It was sad for her,' said Mummy.
'But it did mean that we could adopt you.
And we all wanted you very much.

But first we had to get permission.
We went to see three people
sitting behind a big desk.
They looked rather stern.

They asked us a lot of questions.
Then, at last, they said we could
take you home.

I gave Daddy a big hug!

Always remember that Daddy and I chose you because we wanted you.
Nobody else was good enough.

You and Sue are just as important
as each other.
And Daddy and I love you both just the same.'

Steve felt very proud.
Not many children were chosen
by their family.
He felt like rushing out
and telling all his friends.

Instead, he picked up Rags
and gave him a cuddle.
'It's nice to feel wanted, isn't it?'
he said.

The End